E
YEE   Yee, Wong Herbert
        The Officer's ball.

The Officers' Ball

Wong Herbert Yee

Houghton Mifflin Company
Boston 1997

To Margaret Raymo,
for inviting me to the dance

For information about this and other Houghton Mifflin
trade and reference books and multimedia products, visit
The Bookstore at Houghton Mifflin on the World Wide Web
at http://www.hmco.com/trade.

The text of this book is set in 14 point Times Ten.
The illustrations are watercolor, reproduced in full color.

Library of Congress Cataloging-in-Publication Data

Yee, Wong Herbert.
The Officers' Ball / Wong Herbert Yee.
p. cm.
Summary: Although Sergeant Hippo is nervous about
attending the Officers' Ball, the practice he has done
while on duty pays off at the dance.
ISBN 0-395-81182-1
[1. Dancing — Fiction. 2. Police — Fiction.
3. Animals — Fiction. 4. Stories in rhyme.]
I. Title. PZ8.3.Y42Of 1997
[E] — dc20 96-13718 CIP AC

Manufactured in the United States of America
WOZ 10 9 8 7 6 5 4 3 2 1

In the police station, up on the wall,
Hangs a poster for the Officers' Ball.
When invitations arrive in the mail,
Sergeant Hippo turns ghostly pale.

The card says:

Dinner and Dance — bring a friend.
P.S. — Officers MUST attend.

While his partner is walking their beat,
Hippo sneaks off to see Madame Lafeet.

"ONE-two-three-ONE-two-three
Round the dance floor,
ONE-two-three-ONE-two-three
Try it once more!"

The music plays at three-quarter time.

Good thing stomping hoofs is no crime.

While struggling to learn the fandango
Down at the corner, two taxis tango!
The sergeant hustles past Madame Lafeet,
Scoots down the fire escape to the street.

He directs traffic off to the right
Still daydreaming of the dance that night.

"*ONE-two-three-ONE-two-three*
Keep to the right,
ONE-two-three-ONE-two-three
Go on green light."
Once the accident's under control,
Hippo heads out on highway patrol.

An old pickup truck rumbles past,
Spewing smoke and driving too fast.
As the sergeant writes out a citation,
The dispatcher calls from the station:

"All units to Farmer Pig's farm . . .
A burglar has tripped the alarm!"
Sergeant Hippo revs up his bike,
And takes off down the turnpike.

The sergeant finds an unwelcome guest
Plucking a chicken right from her nest.

He collars and handcuffs the crook,
Frees the hens that the burglar took.
While his partner grabs all the glory,
Sergeant Hippo takes inventory.

"ONE-two-three-ONE-two-three
White, brown, and black,
ONE-two-three-FOUR-five-six
Hens in the sack."

"Come quick!" cries Farmer Pig's neighbor.
"Mother Rabbit's gone into labor!"
Into the wagon hops Father and Mother,
Sixteen sisters and only one brother.

Sergeant Hippo calls in to report,
"Will be providing police escort."

While in the hospital's waiting room,
Hippo waltzes around with a broom.
"ONE-two-three-ONE-two-three
Turn twist and twirl,
ONE-two-three-ONE-two-three..."
"Look! It's a GIRL!"

After joining a brief celebration,
Sergeant Hippo returns to the station.

He writes up the police report,
Sipping coffee and nibbling a torte.
Oh no! Shift's over. Time for a shower.
The Officers' Ball begins in one hour.

Hippo arrives at the ball by the bay,

Leaves his bicycle with the valet.

Sneaking behind some potted plants,

He rehearses one final dance.

"ONE-two-three-ONE-two-three
Needles and pins,
ONE-two-three-ONE-two-three . . ."
"The ball begins!"

Sergeant Hippo hides behind the punch bowl.

Across the table squirms Officer Mole.

He brushes some crumbs from his pants,

Finds the courage to ask her to dance.

First they cakewalk and bunny hug.

Next a waltz, then the jitterbug.

Do the hokey pokey and boogaloo.

It's disco fever, now break dancing too!

Captain Crocodile shines the spotlight,
Searching for the best dancers that night.
"Allow me to introduce to you all . . .

The king and queen of the Officers' Ball!"

"ONE-two-three-ONE-two-three
Round the dance floor,
ONE-two-three-ONE-two-three . . .
Let's dance some MORE!"